Floppy Friends

GO TO THE BEACH

by
Nancy E. Krulik

ISBN 0-439-10403-3

12 11 10 9 8 7 6 5 4 3 2 1   9/9 0 1 2 3 4/0

Illustrations by Chris Dellorco
Designed by Joan Ferrigno

Printed in the U.S.A.   14

First Scholastic printing, August 1999

Floppy Friends

GO TO THE BEACH

by
Nancy E. Krulik

SCHOLASTIC INC.
New York   Toronto   London   Auckland   Sydney
Mexico City   New Delhi   Hong Kong

CHAPTER one POOR BUSTER

Brrring! Brrring!

The phone rang in Buster's living room, but the bulldog didn't get off the couch to pick it up. Buster was too sad to talk to anybody. He'd just found out that his family was moving, and when September came he'd have to go to a new school. Everyone there would already know one another. Buster *hated* the idea of being the new kid.

Finally Buster's mother answered the phone. "Buster, it's for you," she said. "It's Honey."

Buster brightened — a little. Honey was a friend of his from Camp Thunder Hill. Buster hadn't talked to her, or to any of his other camp friends, since he'd come home from camp the week before.

"Hi, Honey," Buster mumbled as he took the phone from his mother.

"Hi. You sound sad," Honey said. "What's going on?"

"My family's moving," Buster moaned. "I'll have to make all new friends in some strange place. Ugh!"

"But, Buster, you're good at making friends," Honey replied. "Look how many new friends you made at camp."

Buster thought about it. He had come to Camp Thunder Hill without knowing anyone. By the time camp was over, he had lots of new friends.

"And speaking of camp friends, I think it's time for a reunion," Honey continued. "Moe, Dot, Prince, and I are all going to the Ocean City beach this afternoon. Do you want to meet us there?"

"I'm not really in the mood . . ." Buster began.

But Honey was not a bear who took "no" for an answer. "It will cheer you up," she promised. "We'll meet you by the lifeguard's chair at one o'clock."

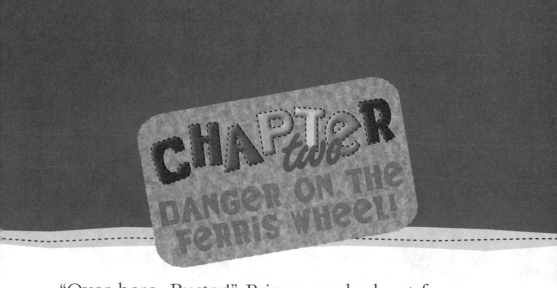

CHAPTER two
DANGER ON THE FERRIS WHEEL!

"Over here, Buster!" Prince croaked out from beneath a big red-and-yellow beach umbrella that was planted right next to the lifeguard's chair.

Buster raced onto the beach. Honey had been right. Just hearing his friend's voice made Buster a little happier. He plopped down onto Moe's beach towel and smiled.

"Hey, guys!" Buster said. "Good to see some familiar faces. Pretty soon, nothing's going to look familiar to me."

Dot smiled and stretched a thin ladybug wing around Buster. "Honey told us you were moving," she said. "That's tough."

"Well, we're not thinking about that today," Honey ordered. "Today we're having fun!" Honey was a take-charge kind of bear. She picked up a big pink sand pail and purple shovel and handed them to Buster. "Let's see if we can build the world's largest sand castle."

The kids all worked together to build the castle. First they made a high tower with spikes along the top. Then they dug a thick moat and filled it with water. It looked fantastic! Finally Buster grabbed a branch with a leaf still attached to it. He stuck the branch into the top of the tower and . . . *crash!* The whole building collapsed into a pile of wet sand.

"Oops!" Buster said, blushing. "Sorry."

Prince hopped up from the sand. "Oh, well," he said. "That just means it's swim time! Last one in the ocean is a rotten egg!" Prince raced down to the waves. His friends followed close behind.

Dot, Buster, Moe, and Prince had a great time riding the waves. Dot and Prince shared a surfboard,

but Buster and Moe did daring tricks on their own boards.

Honey stayed near the shore collecting seashells. At home, Honey had a wonderful collection of shells from a lot of different beaches. Honey was not a great swimmer. She was still a little afraid of the water, but she liked to watch her friends take on the waves.

Eventually Dot, Buster, Moe, and Prince joined Honey near the shore. Buster said, "I'm ready for some *real* excitement!"

"Not me," Prince said. "I want food. Maybe some ice cream or candy."

Honey laughed. Prince was always thinking about food — especially swects! Prince had never met a dessert he didn't like.

"I know where we can eat *and* have some excitement," Moe told the others. "Let's go to the boardwalk!"

"Awesome!" Buster cried out.

"Let's go!" Dot agreed.

There was so much to see and do on the boardwalk. There were games and rides, restaurants and shops. Honey, Moe, Buster, and Dot didn't know what to do first. But Prince did. He hopped right into the candy store and bought himself a big box of saltwater taffy!

Just then, Dot spotted a stuffed pink poodle hanging from the ceiling of a basketball game booth.

"Boy, that would look so great in my room," Dot declared. "But I'm terrible at basketball. I'm too short to shoot."

"No you're not, Dot," Honey laughed. She picked Dot up and paid fifty cents to the man in the booth.

The man handed Dot a basketball. The little ladybug stared at the basket, adjusted her aim, and took the shot. *Swish!* The ball went right into the basket!

"Score!" Honey shouted out. She was so excited she almost dropped Dot!

The man handed the poodle to Dot, and the girls hurried ahead to meet their friends.

"Let's go on the Ferris wheel," Moe suggested. "I heard you can see for miles from the top."

"Nah! Ferris wheels are for babies," Buster said, a little too quickly.

The other kids weren't insulted. They knew all about Buster. Whenever he was really scared of something, he made fun of it.

"Come on, Buster. It'll be fun!" Dot urged.

Buster nodded, took a deep breath, and followed
his pals over to the giant wheel. The five friends
piled into a red car and waited for the ride operator

to throw the switch. Finally the ca...
Up, up, up it went. Buster covered h...
couldn't look. He hated heights.

The others were happy to look out ov...
ocean. "I'll bet you can see clear to the oth...
of the world from here," Prince said as he too...
bite of blue taffy.

Suddenly the ride stopped. The kids waited for...
to start up again, but it didn't. Something was wrong...
with the Ferris wheel. It wasn't moving. And their
red car was stuck at the top!

"Oh, no!" Buster cried out. This was more
excitement than he had bargained for! "We're stuck
up here. Help! HELP!" Buster flailed his arms wildly.
The red car rocked back and forth.

Moe peered over the side of the car. Almost
immediately he discovered what had happened.
A woman's red towel was jammed into one of
the gears.

"Don't worry, Buster. I'll save us," Moe assured
his friend. He started to climb out of the red car.

Buster looked down. Yikes! They were at least
twenty stories off the ground! If Moe slipped and
fell . . . Buster didn't even want to *think* about
what would happen.

"Moe! Don't!" Buster cried out.

But it was too late. Moe was already out of the
car and hanging from the metal spokes of the Ferris
wheel.

started to move.
is eyes. He
er the
er side
k a
it

CHAPTER three
WHERE DID MOE GO?

Moe reached down and grabbed onto the metal bar below the red car. Then, ever so slowly, he used his long arms and legs to bravely climb down toward the gearbox.

Finally Moe reached the center of the wheel. He held onto the metal bar with his left hand and yanked at the red towel with his right.

"Moe, hold on tight!" Buster cried out from high above.

Moe moved the towel back and forth until it was freed from the gears. He held the towel high in the air and raised it like a flag.

"I got it! I got it!" Moe cried up to his friends. Then he scampered down to the ground and told the ride operator that the Ferris wheel was ready to go.

As the red car made its way toward the ground, Buster was excited. He couldn't wait to get off and congratulate Moe. (Actually he couldn't wait to get off, period!) Moe was a real hero. He'd saved them all.

Finally the ride operator opened the door of the red car. Buster, Prince, Dot, and Honey leaped out.

"Moe! That was the most awesome —" Buster shouted out. He stopped in midsentence. Moe was nowhere to be found.

"Hey! Where did Moe go?" Buster asked the others.

"I don't know," Honey replied. "I figured he'd be waiting here for us."

"Maybe he went back to the beach," Dot suggested.

"Let's go find him," Prince said as he hopped off toward the sand.

The kids trudged along in the hot sand until they reached their beach umbrella. They looked for Moe, but they couldn't find him anywhere.

"I wonder where he could have gone," Dot said.

"Maybe he went for a swim," Prince suggested. "He probably worked up a real sweat climbing on that Ferris wheel. I'll go look for him!"

And with that, Prince grabbed his surfboard and ran toward the waves. The others watched as he paddled out into the ocean. They stared at the waves until they could no longer see the frog.

"What do you want to do now?" Dot asked.

"Prince will probably be back pretty soon," Honey replied. "So we'd better not go anywhere. Why don't we try to rebuild the sand castle while we wait?" Buster nodded in agreement. He picked up a bucket, filled it with wet sand, and carefully turned it over. Dot grabbed a shovel and began building a moat.

The three friends were having so much fun that they hardly realized how much time had passed. But now the castle was finished. And Prince had still not returned.

"Now where did *Prince* go?" Buster asked nervously.

CHAPTER *four*

COULD IT BE QUICKSAND?

Buster looked down the beach. In the distance he saw a few high sand dunes.

"Maybe Prince surfed over that way and went ashore to look for Moe," Buster suggested, pointing toward the dunes.

Dot shrugged. "It seems as good a place as any to look," she said.

"We don't have any better ideas," Honey agreed. She started walking toward the dunes.

The sun was high in the sky, and the sand was very hot. "I'm pretty thirsty," Buster complained.

"It's kind of funny," Dot said as she pointed toward the ocean. "Look at all that water. And we have nothing to drink."

"Salt water would taste awful. Too much salt can ruin anything," Buster remarked.

Honey and Dot frowned. They were remembering a trick Buster had played on Moe while they were at camp. Buster had loosened the top of the saltshaker. When Moe went to add a little salt to his soup, a whole pile of it landed in his bowl. Buster had spent half the summer playing practical jokes, and he was the only one who ever thought they were funny.

Finally Honey, Dot, and Buster reached the dunes. Buster climbed to the top of a hill on the left. Honey climbed the highest dune. Dot mounted the smallest dune.

"I don't see Prince anywhere," Honey cried out from the top of her sand dune.

"Me either," Dot called back. "How about you, Buster?"

There was no answer.

"Buster, do you see him?" Honey shouted again.

But Buster did not reply.

"Come on, Buster, quit kidding around!" Honey insisted.

There was still no sound coming from the sand dune on the left.

Quickly Honey raced toward the dune. Dot scurried to meet her. As they reached the top, the girls discovered that Buster was no longer standing on the hill. Could he be hiding? The girls looked behind some brush. They looked down on the beach below. But Buster wasn't anywhere to be found.

Just then, Dot spotted a blue baseball cap in the sand.

"Is — isn't that Buster's cap?" she stammered nervously.

Honey didn't say anything. She just gulped and nodded.

"You don't think Buster got swallowed up by some quicksand or something, do you?" Dot asked. She moved away from the baseball cap just in case. She didn't want to be swallowed up by the hot brown sand the way Buster seemed to have been.

Just then, Honey saw something move in the sand. It was little and white and looked remarkably like a puppy's toe. A *bulldog* puppy's toe!

Honey silently pointed toward the toe and smiled. Dot nodded. They knew where Buster was. He was playing a trick on them. Now it was the girls' turn to play one on him.

"Well, I guess there's just one thing to do," Honey said loudly. "Let's just sit here on this mound of sand and wait. . . ."

As Honey pretended to plop down right about where Buster's belly would be, the mound of sand moved out of the way. Dot reached over and yanked up the baseball cap. There was Buster! He had buried himself in the sand up to his neck and covered his face with his cap.

"Gotcha!" Buster cried out.

Honey and Dot could not believe it.

"Buster? What are you doing? How you can play jokes at a time like this? Our two friends are missing!" Honey growled.

"You know me," Buster defended himself. "There's no time too scary for a practical joke!"

"We know you, all right," Honey sighed. "And for some reason, we like you anyway."

"I guess Moe and Prince aren't here," Dot said, trying to change the subject before Honey and Buster started arguing. "Where should we look now?"

"How about the snack bar?" Buster suggested. "We could look for them there and get ourselves something to drink."

Even Honey had to admit that was a good idea. So the three friends headed away from the sand dunes and back toward the boardwalk.

"I'm going to get some ice cream," Dot said. "Something cold and creamy would hit the spot right now."

Honey licked her lips. "Sounds good to me," she agreed. "How about you, Buster?"

Buster shook his head. "I'm going to that lemonade stand over there. I'll meet you guys by the ice-cream shop."

Buster walked to the lemonade stand. The woman at the stand took his money and handed him a tall, cool glass of lemonade. Buster took a sip, turned, and started walking toward the ice-cream store. He looked in the window. Suddenly his stomach felt as though a million butterflies were dancing inside. Something was terribly wrong.

The ice-cream shop was closed. And Honey and Dot had disappeared. Buster was all alone at the beach!

CHAPTER five
ATTACK OF THE CAVE MONSTER!

Buster wanted to cry. Now he knew exactly how he was going to feel on the first day in his new school. He was going to be scared and all alone. It was a terrible, horrible, yucky feeling!

But Buster didn't have time to feel sorry for himself right now. His friends had all disappeared. They could be in trouble and waiting for Buster to save them.

Buster walked quickly back down toward the beach. He looked around for any sign of Honey and Dot. He didn't see the girls, but he did discover two sets of footprints in the sand. One set was very large. One set was teeny tiny. Those footprints could only belong to Honey and Dot.

As Buster began following the footprints, his mind was racing with horrible thoughts. What if his friends had been captured by space aliens? Or what if they were prisoners on an evil pirate's ship?

Buster followed the footprints for as long as he could. The prints came to a sudden stop outside a dark cave. Oh, no! This was worse than anything Buster could have imagined. Buster knew what kind of horrible creatures lived in the caves of Ocean City. His big cousin Spike had told him scary stories about them. Spike said the caves were filled with angry sea monsters that breathed fire and captured small children so they could barbecue them and eat them for dinner. It was the sea monster's revenge on all the people who ate crabs, shrimp, clams, and lobsters.

Just then, Buster saw a bright light coming from inside the cave. The monster was breathing fire! Buster wanted to scream and run away. He wanted to go home right then. But Buster didn't run. Instead, he inched toward the cave. He had to face the monster. He had to save his friends!

CHAPTER six
SURPRISE!

As Buster took his first step into the cave, the light went out. Buster became even more frightened. Was the monster trying to trick him? Was he going to grab him in the dark?

"Honey? Dot?" Buster whispered nervously into the darkness. "Moe? Prince? Are you guys in here?"

There was no answer. Buster took another frightened step into the cave. Suddenly there was a huge flash of light. But it wasn't monster fire that lit the cave. It was flashlights. Four flashlights. And each one belonged to one of Buster's friends.

"SURPRISE!" Moe, Prince, Honey, and Dot shouted.

"This time *we* got you!" Honey added.

Buster gulped and stared at his friends. "Why . . . how . . . what?" he stammered helplessly.

"It's a party to celebrate that you're moving," Moe explained.

Buster frowned. "That's not anything to celebrate," he said.

"It is if you are moving to a really great town with very friendly kids," Dot told him.

"How do you know my new town is so great?" Buster barked at her.

"Because I just moved there last week," Dot told him. "You're moving to Cloverdale. Your mom told my mom about it when they were up at camp on visiting day."

"And guess who else lives in Cloverdale," Prince said to Buster.

"Who?" Buster replied.

"We do!" shouted Prince, Moe, and Honey.

"You mean we'll all be together in school?" Buster asked as a big smile flashed across his face.

"That's what it means, pal!" Honey told him. "I promised you this trip to the beach would cheer you up."

Buster laughed. "You were right about that," he told her. "But why didn't you guys just tell me? You knew how scared I was about moving."

"Oh, you know us," Honey told him. "There's no time too scary for a practical joke."

Buster couldn't argue with that. In fact, he was too happy to argue about anything. Buster couldn't wait to move into his new house. He had a feeling this was going to be the best school year ever!